THE BIGGEST BED IN THE WORLD

LINDSAY CAMP

illustrated by

JONATHAN LANGLEY

HarperCollins*Publishers*

When Ben was a baby, he liked
to sleep in his mom and dad's bed.

At first, it was fine.

But, as Ben grew bigger, the problems began.

"How am I supposed to sleep like this?" said Ben's dad.

Ben's dad tried sleeping in Ben's bed,

but that was even worse.

So Ben's dad went to the store

and bought a bigger bed.

At first, the new bed was better.

But then . . .

Ben's baby brother, Billy, was born.

"How am I supposed to sleep like this?" said Ben's dad.

So he went back to the store

and bought the biggest bed they had.

At first, this bed was much better.

But then . . .

the twins, Beth and Bart, were born,

and the problems began all over again.

"Oh no!" groaned Ben's dad.

Then he had an idea.

He bought a lot of wood, and took it upstairs.

He hammered and crashed and banged

until he'd built . . .

the **biggest** bed in the world.
It was enormous! The bed was so big, he had to knock
down several walls to make enough room for it.

"There," said Ben's dad, putting down his hammer.

"Now I should be able to get some sleep."

And he was right.

The bed was big enough for all the family to sleep comfortably.

Even after the triplets,
Brittany, Bella, and Boris,
arrived.

But the biggest bed in the world

was also the heaviest bed in the world.

And knocking down the walls had

made the house rather weak and wobbly.

So, in the middle of the night . . .

Down,

Down,

Down

went the bed.

Faster
and
Faster

until . . .

Faster
and
Faster
and

SPLA

"HEY!" said Ben's dad. "How am I supposed to sleep like this?"

So Ben's mom and dad went back to sleeping

in an ordinary bed.

And Ben's dad banned Ben and Billy, and

Beth and Bart, and Brittany, Bella, and Boris from the bed.

"Now I'm sure to get a good night's sleep," he said.

But did he?

No. The ordinary bed was a very nice bed,

and very comfortable too.

But somehow, it seemed . . . well, a little empty.

Ben's dad lay awake, tossing and turning, for hours.

"How am I supposed to sleep like this?" he moaned.

"I'll never get to sleep."

But in the end, he did.

For all the children who've ever
slept with a foot in my ear.
—L.C.

For Toby, Holly, and Rosita,
who all loved the "big one bed".
—J.L.

The Biggest Bed in the World
Text copyright © 1999 by Lindsay Camp
Illustrations copyright © 1999 by Jonathan Langley
Printed in Hong Kong. All rights reserved.
http://www.harperchildrens.com
First published in the United Kingdom by HarperCollins Publishers Ltd., 1999

1 2 3 4 5 6 7 8 9 10
❖
First U.S. edition, HarperCollins Publishers Inc., 2000

ISBN 0-06-028687-3
Library of Congress Catalog Card Number 99-61184